Keep The obews
Alive

THE LEGEND OF
CARBUNCLE POND

Robert James Racicot

ISBN-13: 978-1490565743

ISBN-10: 1490565744

This is a work of fiction. Names, characters, places and incidents either are the product of the author's imagination or are used fictitiously, and any resemblance to actual persons, living or dead, events, or locales is entirely coincidental.

This book is dedicated to
my Nana, Doris Moore.
My real blood connection
to the Nipnets

Marvelous as these methods of signaling may seem, there were medicine men who claimed that they could send their thoughts through the air and make things come to pass afar. Others could send their mind's eyes to distant places and discover what was happening. White explorers have written of these things, but to say just how it was done must remain for modern medicine men to tell us.

Arthur C. Parker,
The Indian How Book, 1927

CHAPTER 1

The Earth is the Mother of all people, and all people should have equal rights upon it. You might as well expect the rivers to run backward as that any man who was born a free man should be contented when penned up and denied liberty to go where he pleases.

Joseph
(Hinmaton Yalatki, 1830-1904)
Nez Perce Chief

"But, Dad."

"No 'buts' about it.   You know these stories are made up. The older kids in school are just trying to scare you. Besides, you know it's time you had a job. I had a job at your age, and Stephen had the same job and he never had any trouble."

"Yes, sir," I surrendered.   The twisted distortion on my face showed my true feelings but there was no arguing with my father. Once he made a decision, he stuck with it. My father was real big on teaching us the value of money at an early age and how hard work will pay off someday. Send me to any early grave was more like it.

The job was a paper route — my first real paying job, other than the occasional allowance I got for cutting grass, shoveling snow and trash duty. I inherited the paper route from my older brother Stephen, the Viking. Stephen was erroneously delivered to my parents in AD 1950. He was supposed to have been delivered to a Viking family around AD 950 somewhere on the coast of Norway. But fate screwed up with the delivery date and placed the number one in front. He is the reincarnation of the famous Viking warrior Eric the Red. He was a mammoth, three times bigger than all the other kids in the neighborhood, with a mean-spirited, redheaded temper to match. He enjoyed bullying people and he especially enjoyed picking on me.

A paper route would not normally scare a twelve-year-old kid. In fact, most would be excited about the opportunity. But this paper route was not your average paper route. This paper route included the top of Forest Hill Road, and Injun Joe lived at the top of Forest Hill Road. Once you crossed the railroad tracks you entered Injun Joe land. Every kid in school had heard the stories about Injun Joe, stories of kids disappearing, never to be found. These tales kept you awake at night, afraid that Injun Joe would come down into your neighborhood and abduct you in your sleep. And we believed every word.

The most common story floating around the town's elementary school was that Injun Joe ate kids, slowly roasting them like curly-tailed pigs with apples stuck in their mouths over an outdoor barbecue pit. No one ever found the bodies. No one ever found the bones. He threw the scraps to his part pit bull, part wolverine, part Velociraptor dogs.

"Have you ever seen Injun Joe?" I asked the Viking once.

He roared his Viking war laugh and punched me in the arm. "He's going to eat you," he would say.

The bottom line was that no one goes into Injun Joe country and lives to tell about it. That is, except Stephen, I guess. But he was different. Stephen was big and mean and a Viking. Only Stephen could have survived delivering newspapers up Forest Hill.

"What are you going to do?" my next door neighbor and best friend Jimmy asked when I told him the news.

"I don't know."

"Do you have to go up the hill?"

"Yeah, I have to deliver the paper to his house. My father said I have to do it. He said Stephen did it at my age, and so could I."

"But. . . what about Injun Joe?" Jimmy asked.

"My father said the stories aren't true."

"Yeah, right," Jimmy assured me.

The neighborhood gang cringed at the thought of me riding my bike up the long, steep, frost-heaved, pockmarked road to the top of Forest Hill, never to be seen again. I was doomed. My fate was sealed and all avenues of escape had been closed off. The job was mine. I tried to enjoy my last taste of freedom, the last days of my summer and of my life before I left my youthful world.

CHAPTER 2

The voice of the Great Spirit is heard in the
twittering of birds, the rippling of mighty waters,
and the sweet breathing of flowers. If this is
Paganism, then at present, at least, I am a Pagan.

Gertrude Simmons Bonnin
(Zitkala-Sa, 1876-1938)
Dakota Sioux

The Tuesday after Labor Day weekend was my first day. I would be delivering the paper after school each day and on Saturday mornings. An adult delivered the much larger Sunday paper by car. I couldn't focus on anything during the first day back at school. I couldn't share in the excitement the other kids experienced seeing everyone from town and telling stories of their summer vacations. I just stared out the window counting the minutes ticking away to my fate. The day dragged on like watching grass grow.

The gods, maybe the same ones that had screwed up the Viking's delivery date, had sent a pewter foggy mist that day. An early fall, soaking cold, New England mist, a slow silent weeping for the death of yet another young boy mist. I was being sacrificed to Injun Joe and all the gods could do was cry about it. All I could think was that a Tuesday was a terrible day to die, but then again, when you think about it, any day is probably a terrible day to die.

I picked up the bundle of papers at the end of our street—forty-three, to be exact. The newspaper office had given me a brand new canvas bag that hung around my shoulder to hold the papers while I rode my bike. The Viking had destroyed his. I wrapped each paper with a rubber band to hold it sturdy so I could throw it at the houses' front doors. But, if it was raining, I had to walk up to each house and place the paper inside a screen door or enclosed porch to ensure it stayed dry. The first part of the route was as easy as apple pie and ice cream since it was almost a perfect circle. I started and ended in the same place, except for one small part.

Before I could head west toward safety, I had to head east across the railroad tracks and up Forest Hill Road.

The rule we were taught at a young age from the older kids in the neighborhood was simple. You did not cross the railroad tracks. This is Injun Joe country. The tracks were the boundary to our otherwise perfect kids' outdoor paradise.

Our neighborhood abutted a cemetery, which provided the ideal kick-the-can site on new moon summer nights, hiding amongst the century-old headstones, wondering if a skeleton's hand would reach up out of the ground and grab you by the leg. We challenged each other to sit on the large granite cross in the center of the cemetery guarding all those unwise enough to enter at night. The story we believed was that if you sat real quiet on the cross you could feel it move. Beyond the cemetery were the woods. This was where we built tree forts, played army and cowboys and Indians. At the end of the woods were the railroad tracks. We never ever ventured any further beyond those tracks.

I had practiced the paper route the week before, memorized each house that was my responsibility, except for the last part. Today I had to actually go up there, and because the gods were crying, I had to walk up to each house that did not have a covered stoop at its door. There were only four houses on this part of the route. Injun Joe's was the last. The only times I had ever crossed the tracks and gone up Forest Hill were with my father when we brought our trash to the town dump, several miles beyond Injun Joe's land. When the Viking came with us on the dump trips he would never miss the chance to point out where Injun Joe lived and tell me how he was going to sneak down at night and steal me out of bed for his next meal.

I should have brought a friend. I could have talked Jimmy into coming with me. But why fill Injun Joe's stomach with the flesh of two kids?

I realized it was not a good idea, after all. If I was going to do this, I was going to do it alone.

My brother had done it, Viking or not, and I could do it.

I slowly started the long trek up the steep hill. I eventually had to get off my bike and push.

The first house was about halfway up the hill. It looked abandoned. The weeds in the front yard towered up to my waist. The front of the house looked like a dead man's face with black shutterless windows that gaped out at me. A doorless entryway waited to consume those unwise enough to enter into its black void. One look sent shivers down my spine. Time had taken its toll on this house and then forgotten it and left it to rot. The house inhabited itself and now had a mind all its own. I hoped no one lived there now.

I took out the route book the newspaper office had given me listing the names, addresses and phone numbers of each of my customers to keep track of who had paid and who owed me money. I looked for this house's number but found nothing. Relief flooded my frightened heart. This house was not part of my route. No one lived here but the demon ghosts of Father

Time. I didn't have to answer its beckoning call. I was safe, for now.

As I started to slide the book into my back pocket, I froze. There it was, staring right back out at me. The name—it had never crossed my mind until this very moment—the name given to Injun Joe by the newspaper office. It was there, plain as day, written on the page right before me. The name given to Injun Joe was Joseph Nipnet.

Nipnet, what a strange name. What is a Nipnet?

I had never heard of any Nipnets from town. The thought pushed me on. I slid the book into my back pocket and continued pushing my bike up the hill.

The next house wasn't much better than the last. The only difference I could see at first glance was that this house had evidence of people living in it. It was becoming apparent to me that progress had stood still on Forest Hill Road. The people here had become trapped in some kind of time warp and were forced - or chose - to live in a time long separated from the rest of town. Stephen had never said a word about this place. Then again, he never said much to me about anything except, "I'm going to pound you."

How could a whole part of a modern-day town be forgotten by time?

Then another alarming thought hit me—like I needed more terrors haunting my tortured soul.

How can these other people be living on Injun Joe land? Why has he not eaten them all by now? Unless....unless they are part of his tribe? Maybe they're working for him, capturing kids and turning them over to him as payment to live in peace?

This new idea did not help my psyche. But somehow at this point I switched into autopilot. The surreal mixture of terror, wonder and confusion forced my free will to act all on its own, detached from my brain, as if I was watching myself from outside my body.

As I laid my bike down by the side of the road, dogs barked from somewhere in the back of the next house. I only hoped they were chained. I slowly walked toward the front door and stopped about halfway up. I felt I was stepping back into time. The yard was strewn with junk— rusting metal parts of cars and tractors, stuff that I didn't even recognize, junk from an era long gone by. I didn't need to go any further. The front door had an open covered stoop and my job would be done when the paper hit it.

But, just as I grabbed a paper from my sack and was winding my arm back for the throw, a woman appeared at the door. She spooked me out of my shoes. I jumped back, almost falling. I should have turned and run, screaming at the top of my lungs that the people of Forest Hill were coming to capture all the kids in town for Injun Joe to eat. But I couldn't move another inch. I was frozen in time myself. I stared at her, barely breathing. She looked old, yet strong. She was solid and stout with the kind of strength that comes with eking a living out of the earth. She could have picked me up and snapped me in half right across her knee. She spoke to me in a firm, powerful voice, an aged voice from the past.

"Are you the paper boy?" Her opened mouth displayed a patchwork of greenish brown, craggy teeth interspersed with black cavernous holes of nothing.

I couldn't answer. I was frozen in fear.

"Speak up, boy. What's the matter, cat got your tongue?"

My tongue, she wants my tongue. She wants to boil my tongue and stick it in a pickle jar and place it on the fireplace mantle as a souvenir of yet another boy captured and consumed.

She stepped out of the house and started walking toward me. I should have run, but I was frozen stiff. She stepped up to me. "Give me the paper, boy," she demanded, grabbing the paper out of my hand and nearly lifting me off the ground. She acted like she had no time to waste in a place that time had already forgotten.

"What happened to that big, redheaded kid?" she asked.

My brother. She was asking about my brother, the Viking. The thought of the Viking suddenly gave me the courage to speak.

"He doesn't deliver anymore. I took the route," I responded.

"Well, are you going to collect money for the paper, because he never did? He used to just throw the paper at the house and never once stopped to collect the money."

What do you mean? He never collected money for the paper? The Viking never stopped at the house?

I was dumbfounded. Slowly stuttering, I answered, "Yes, I collect on Fridays."

"Okay," she answered, "we should pay for the paper anyway. We've been getting it free for years now. But why go and complain when it was free?"

She turned without a moment's hesitation and walked back into the house. I stood there for what seemed like eternity, wondering what that was all about.

The Viking had never collected money for the papers?

He delivered the paper for free, so the people wouldn't complain about not getting a paper to the main office, but he never stopped. He just heaved them at the house as he pedaled past, probably riding as fast as he could and praying that no one would capture him.

The Viking was scared of these people. That must be it, plain and simple.

This thought gave me new strength. It rejuvenated my soul. I had crossed the tracks, traveled up the hill and faced one of the people of Forest Hill Road and had survived. She was no less than three feet from me, and I wasn't captured and eaten. I rode up the hill with renewed vigor. I confidently strode up to each of the next two houses. They looked the same—weather beaten, worn and spooky—but that didn't stop me. I walked up to each one and placed the paper inside its screen door. Then I walked—yes, walked—back to my bike. My ego was soaring until reality set in, again. The last house on the route was Injun Joe's — Joseph Nipnet's.

CHAPTER 3

Among the Indians there have been no written laws. Customs handed down from generation to generation have been the only laws to guide them. Every one might act different from what was considered right if he chose to do so, but such acts would bring upon him the censure of the nation. This fear of the Nation's censure acted as a mighty band, binding all in one social, honorable compact.

George Copway
(Kahgegagahbowh, 1818-1863)
Ojibwa Chief

The problem was that Injun Joe didn't actually live on Forest Hill Road. He lived down this very dark looking dirt driveway. The address was classified as Forest Hill because this road had no name. It was just a long, winding, weed-strewn, rutted path. I couldn't just stand back from the safety of the road and heave the paper toward his house. I had to travel into the woods.

The Viking must have traveled down this road, at least. He had to have gotten the paper to the house, even if he didn't collect any money on Fridays. Injun Joe would have complained to the paper office if he didn't get his paper, right?

I started down the road, walking my bike. The further I ventured, the darker it became. The forest on each side of the road grew thicker. The underbrush was thick enough to hide someone only a few feet from the edge of the road. Anyone could lurk here, leap out and grab an unsuspecting victim in an instant. The late afternoon sun was beginning its descent behind the tall pines and oaks. Though, I couldn't see the sky beyond the canopy of trees that stretched over the road.

I didn't see any signs of a house. Up ahead the road curved off to the right and prevented me from seeing what lay ahead. My mind was full of all the horrid stories. My heart was full of all the haunted curses that plagued the vivid imagination of a twelve-year-old boy, and pumped, ever faster, in my chest.

I don't want to die. I am too young to die. I haven't experienced any of life's true rewards.

Yet, I continued. Something deep inside pushed me on. On my first day of the job, I had already accomplished more than my bully brother the Viking. I could get this done. I was soaked to the bone, shivering from the steady, penetrating, god-crying mist, shivering from the fear in my soul.

I reached the corner, and there stood the habitat of Joseph Nipnet. The house was not a house at all. It was a trailer, a small dinosaur-old recreational vehicle that had been dumped there ages ago by an errant traveler. It was more like a camp. A rock-lined cook fire lay in the middle. Blue and green tarps were strung across trees around the edges of the camp covering boxes of things and firewood. An old, rusted-out, pockmarked, tireless pickup truck rested on cement blocks, now a prisoner to the entwining grape vines. I didn't see the remains of any human bones in the fire pit, though even if I had seen any bones I'm sure I wouldn't have been able to tell the difference between human and animal. I also didn't see any shrunken human heads hanging in the trees or the remains of wayward travelers who had been looking for directions. Actually, the place looked cool, like the hippie camp that my friends and I had seen in the endless woods and trails of our town.

Our town had flooded twice in the 1950s, so the Army Corps of Engineers took over half the land and built two dams along the French River. That land became an outdoor man's paradise. In the summer, we rode mini bikes with dreams of graduating to the Viking's Bridgestone 100 dirt bike someday. My father took us snowmobiling in the winter. In the fall, you could hear the hunters' shotguns blasting away at whatever moved in the woods. But last summer, for the first time, we saw a gypsy caravan of hippies drive into the woods. We watched them from afar as they attempted to live off the land. The camp looked cool, but it wasn't long before they packed up and moved on. I didn't mention the hippies to the Viking and I told the gang not to mention it to anyone, lest the Viking and his gang of marauders pillage and plunder their camp. Joseph Nipnet's house looked like a cool hippie camp of gypsy wanderers who had forgotten where to go next and stayed.

A dog brought my daydreaming to a quick end. He appeared from under one of the tarps and walked toward the front of the trailer. My heart stopped beating. There standing before me was the largest wolf dog I had ever seen, easily the size of two large dogs combined, two hundred pounds of pure carnivorous power.

He stood his ground like a warrior sentinel guarding his kingdom from unwanted intruders. He licked his chops, displaying long white dagger fangs, in anticipation of his next tasty meal of roasted boy.

"Thanks," I said to no one in particular. "Thanks for the dog and for this bone-chilling mist."

He didn't bark or make any sudden movements toward me. The dog just stood his ground and waited for his next victim to come closer, for the command of his master to come get me and drag me back for dinner.

His next move baffled me. My mouth popped open like the shells of a steamed clam. The wolf dog turned around and went to the side of the trailer and lay down. He just lay there, licking his paw, no longer paying any attention to me. I hadn't heard anyone yell or give a command. I didn't see anything or anyone but the dog.

Where was Injun Joe?

He could have been hiding somewhere near me and I wouldn't have seen him. Something weird was happening. I started to sense a feeling that everything was okay here. The aura of foreboding that had crowded my tormented soul was slowly leaving. A sense of security started creeping in. Telling me it was okay to go further on. I walked on with this new calm feeling, quietly pushing my bike ever closer to Injun Joe's trailer. The front door had a wooden open covering that I could throw the paper under. I stopped at the point where I could reach the covering with a good heave of the paper and let it fly. It landed only a few feet from where the dog was lying. He nonchalantly looked up from his quiet position, as if to say 'thanks.'

I hopped on my bike and pedaled out of the dark tree tunnel. I pedaled away from Injun Joe's place of torture and cannibalism, not feeling scared at all. I was safe. I pedaled at a normal pace. I didn't feel the need to go any faster, to run away. I had faced my worst fears and won. I had conquered my demons. I had made it down Injun Joe's road, had faced his wolf dog, and I had survived. Most importantly, I had done what the Viking had done and lived to tell about it.

CHAPTER 4

The sound is fading away
It is of five sounds
Freedom
The sound is fading away
It is of five sounds

Chippewa Song

The rest of the week was easy and uneventful. I was in my zone. I was a natural at delivering papers. I became a living legend to my awed neighborhood friends. I had delivered the paper to Injun Joe and survived. I'd ventured eastward from our neighborhood bubble, traveled beyond the tracks and survived. I'd traveled up Forest Hill Road and faced the time-forgotten people and survived.

I felt especially salient when the Viking asked me how the paper route was going. I knew he was thinking about his own fears and how he had taken money out of his own profits so he wouldn't have to stop and collect from the houses on Forest Hill.

I proudly smiled back at him and said, "It's great. I love it."

I think he sensed a new strength in me, a new courage. But, of course, he just laughed a Viking laugh and said, "Delivering is one thing, but collecting is another thing all its own. Wait until you have to knock on doors."

I'm sure my response and show of confidence freaked him out. Normally, I would have displayed a face full of fear, but not this time. This time I smiled back at him. His squinted eyes gave me a look of mistrust, as if to ask 'what's up with you?' Then he just punched me in the arm. I had the toughest arms of anyone in town, for I lived taking Viking punches. He didn't know that I knew his secret. The biggest bully of the town, my brother, was a fraud. He was afraid of the people on Forest Hill. I kept his secret to myself for now. Maybe someday I could use it to my advantage. Best not to waste any edge I had over him just yet.

The events that had occurred down Joseph Nipnet's road repeated themselves each day, almost to the letter of some unwritten law of the universe. The wolf dog walked out to the front of the trailer and then lay down when he saw it was me, as if someone was telling him I was okay or he sensed it himself. The papers from the day before were not there, so someone was picking them up. I never saw any sign of Joseph Nipnet. I wasn't thinking of him as Injun Joe anymore. Somehow I sensed he would want it that way.

And then, before I knew it, Friday came. I sat in school staring out the windows contemplating my fate. Several times the teachers called on me and reprimanded me for not paying attention. I had previously told my friends that Friday was payday. I said it not with the excitement of getting paid from my first independent job, but with the sense of foreboding for the coming terror of knocking on Joseph Nipnet's door and asking for payment. When I told my friends, all they could say was, "good luck," and of course, "it's been nice knowing you," which didn't boost my spirits much.

Now wasn't the time for jokes. Even my closest, most trusted friend Jimmy didn't offer to come along. I think this time I would have accepted his help. But I was too proud to ask for it. This was my fate and I had to accept it, eaten or not. Besides, I had started to feel safe there. Every day the wolf dog just lay down and ignored my advances, and every day I inched a little closer to throw the paper.

School ended, and I picked up my stack of forty-three papers, removed the twine holding the bundle together and slid them into the canvas shoulder bag. I jumped on my bike and headed off down Main Street. I had planned out the most efficient route to minimize the time it took me to deliver the papers. I always saved the top of Forest Hill for last and then would sail my bike down the long steep hill for the fast ride back home.

"It's only right to have to pay for the paper," the ancient Amazon warrior said after I knocked on the door of her house.

I arrived at the long dirt trail that led to Joseph's trailer. Today I stopped when I turned the corner and the trailer came into view. I stood there for what seemed like forever. The wolf dog was already lying down and was even further away from the door than usual, as if to say, 'Hey, it's okay. It's safe.' I'm sure he could hear my heart pounding in my chest and smell the fear particles emanating from my nervous skin. He had given me plenty of room to walk past without the worry of him pouncing on my unsuspecting back. Again, a strong feeling of security overwhelmed me. I did feel safe, but...... Maybe this was the guise used by Joe on his unsuspecting victims to draw them into a false sense of security and then ambush them. Somehow I didn't believe that anymore either.

What was giving me this feeling? Where was it coming from?

I neared the closest spot where I'd thrown the paper yesterday and stopped. I took a deep breath then continued on. I reached the front door still feeling safe in my new position. The wolf dog just stayed where he lay looking at me. I reached my arm back to knock. A second before my knuckles hit the door an image caught my eye. I glanced over. There, on the side of the trailer, hanging on a hook was a bow with a quiver of arrows. The bow was long and sturdy with fur wrapped around the wood handle. The quiver was made of a tan and whitish fur with a rawhide strap that hung around the user's shoulders. The arrows inside were fletched with multi-colored feathers. Next to the bow, resting on two hooks was a spear. The head was a sharpened stone, like clear ice, with a razor's edge. The spear had fur wrapped around a wooden shaft, where a warrior would grip the weapon for throwing. Then I noticed that the spear head had a dried brownish, red stain across its surface.

Blood?

My knuckles hit the door.

It opened.

I took a step back in astonishment and gasped out a whisper of, "Huh?"

Towering before me was a real live Indian Chief, straight out of the Western movies we watched on our four-channel, black and white, rabbit-eared television set. Standing before me was Tonto, but much bigger. He was dressed in deerskin from shirt to moccasins with a rawhide belt around his waist and a long buck knife slid into a leather scabbard. On the other side was a throwing tomahawk with a wooden handle and a metal blade. Its head rested in a half-circled slot of rawhide. He had long, silver hair pulled back into a pony tail that ran down his back. His face was etched with deep lines, which bore the wisdom of the ages — the knowledge of all that had passed and all that was still to come. But, the most remarkable thing was his projection of power. He held the stance of a battle-hardened warrior. His hands were the size of my tiny twelve-year-old pin head.

I was frozen. Not in fear, but in awe. Then a glint caught my eye from a small stone hanging around his neck on a piece of rawhide. It was a deep bright red, with a hint of a pinkish orange in the center. Like the pink orange of the sun's rays reflecting off low hanging clouds during a winter sunset. The most amazing thing was its shine, which didn't come from any reflected light bouncing off it. It had a shine all its own, like it had a fire burning inside it.

Joseph gazed down at me, smiled and quickly tucked the stone into his deerskin shirt.

"I have been expecting you," he said in a deep, commanding yet quiet voice.

"Yes, sir, it's payday today. I have to collect for the paper. It's seventy-five cents."

"Yes," he answered and handed me a dollar. I started to reach into my change bag but he gently touched my hand with his massive, calloused, warrior hand and slowly shook his head, as if to say, 'no, you keep the change.'

"Thank you," I said.

"So your older brother Stephen, or should I say the Viking," he said with a smile and a wink, "never collected money for the paper, even when I left it on the front porch in an envelope for him, even when I asked Nepon to stay out of sight so as not to scare him. Years delivering the paper and I don't think that silly boy ever once stepped a foot beyond his paper throwing range."

"Huh?" was all I could get out. I was slack-jawed. My tongue might have hung out of my mouth for all I knew. My head was spinning from information overload, aching like an ice cream brain freeze. Too many questions filled my mind.

How did he know the Viking was my brother? How does he know the nickname I gave him? No one knew that name. And who was Nepon? That must be his wolf dog's name. Did he call the Viking 'silly boy?' Ha, wait until I tell the gang that one.

Joseph laughed, not a Viking pillaging howl which is a familiar sound that echoed through our house, but a wise, discerning, enlightened kind of laugh.

"Um, my brother?" I asked.

As if he knew what I was thinking, he answered my question.

"Yes, I know the other paperboy is your brother, and I know he doesn't treat you nice sometimes."

What do you mean 'sometimes?'

"But, I also know he is a coward," Joseph added with a big smile across his caverned face of ancient knowledge.

I didn't know what to say. I was stumped.

The Viking was a coward?

Here was confirmation from an adult who emanated all the wisdom of the world, and more, from a real live Indian warrior.

Maybe it was true. The Viking never collected money from anyone on Forest Hill, even Injun Joe, or Joseph Nipnet. Injun Joe was a derogatory and disrespectful name toward this warrior chief.

The Viking's cowardice was getting to be a common thread in my real knowledge of him, the classic bully coward syndrome.

Maybe, just once, if I stood up to him, he might back down.

Joseph stepped out of his trailer. He gestured toward the chairs that were set up around his cook fire, the same fire pit every kid in town knew for a fact was the site where he cooked his captured victims.

"Can you sit a minute, and meet Nepon?" he asked.

My stranger danger alert flag should have shot up. Even in 1969, we were warned about strangers and their ploy to kidnap a victim using cute, friendly animals as a ruse. But, even more now, I felt safe here. A real Indian Chief couldn't be any danger. Maybe back in the early days of our country, maybe in the fight for our westward expansion, but not in 1969.

So, I walked over to the fire pit and took a seat. His wolf dog—Nepon—waited for Joseph to come and join me. When he sat, Nepon stood, walked to him and laid his massive wolf head in Joseph's lap.

"He wants to meet you. Can he come over? He won't bite," Joseph said.

"Yes," I said.

Without a word from Joseph, Nepon quietly, gently walked over to me. His head bent down not in a sign of submission, but of saying, "I am not a threat to you."

I reached out my hand. He licked it. Then he slid his massive head onto my lap and let me pet his lion-thick, silver mane. His fur was the softest material I had ever laid my hands on, like fluffy snow. His body felt like a massive statue of muscle.

"His name is Nepon. It means 'spirit friend,'" Joseph said.

"Hi, Nepon," I said. He lifted his eyes toward me. They were the bluest blue I had ever seen; they were the ocean's morning sky before the sweltering summer sun climbed and blistered its worshipers below. They were the blue of the blueberries we picked on Cemetery Hill next to our neighborhood. But, the most amazing thing was that the pupils were the same faint, pinkish orange hue of a sunset after a hot July day. The same color as the center of the stone I had seen around Joseph's neck.

Then he smiled at me. I swear to you this day, I have seen other dogs smile in their own way, but this was a real smile.

"He likes you," Joseph said.

"Yes," was all I could say, with a huge grin. I was in complete rapture. I was now friends with the most fierce and vicious, yet soft and gentle giant of a dog. I liked animals. I still do, of course.

Our family hadn't gotten a new dog since our last one, Blackie, was hit by a car crossing Main Street at night. I rode with my father to the veterinarian that night, sitting in the back seat with Blackie lying across my body, as he whined in pain. I patted him and tried to comfort him as best I could, crying to myself and telling him over and over again, "It's okay, Blackie. You're going to be okay, Blackie."

Blackie didn't come home with us that night. I still miss him. He was our faithful companion. He was one of the gang. He followed us everywhere, every day, trampling through the woods, swimming in the pond, and to the anguish of my mother, sloshing through the muddy swamps of the sand pit.

"Your brother believes the stories about me, and I sense you do too."

I opened my mouth to say something, to deny the accusation. But Joseph smiled and raised his hand to me, stopping me from making a fool of myself or lying to him.

"But still, despite all you believed, you faced your fears, defeated them and knocked on my door. That shows courage. Heroes show courage and conquer their fears," he said with another perceptive smile.

Hero? I knew I was no hero.

"I don't believe them now," I lied.

He laughed his wise laugh, as if he knew I was lying. "That is good."

Then he said, like he knew my schedule, like he knew everything about me, "It is getting late. You probably should be going. Your mother will be worried if you are late, and your father will surely be upset if you are late for dinner."

How did he know about my father's strict policy of never being late for dinner? And he knew what everyone said about him, all this while living at the top of Forest Hill, alone, in the woods. I had never seen him come into town. Surely someone would have noticed a full-fledged Indian Chief dressed in buckskins around town. No one had ever talked of seeing him come into town, except, of course, the Viking, who told me he would steal me away in the night. He lived off the land, like his ancestors. And yet he knew everything that went on in town. How?

"Okay," I said and stood to go. Nepon had lain down at my feet, content to be close and listen. He stood when I stood.

"Michael, do you want to bring your friends here? I have a story I would like to tell you and them about Carbuncle Pond, but when we have more time. Besides, I want to show them that I don't eat kids. How about on Saturday after you deliver the morning paper?"

I was stumped, again. But I was intrigued at the thought of Joseph Nipnet–Chief Nipnet–telling us a story, especially one about the pond across the street from our neighborhood.

Carbuncle Pond was already a special place for us. We took swimming lessons at the beach on weekday summer mornings. The water became very deep, very fast, and reached depths over your head only twenty feet from the shore. You could buy candy and cheeseburgers at the concession stand. There was a raft further out that the Viking ruled in his game of King of the Raft, pushing anyone else off that tried to stand on it. We remembered hearing stories from the older kids in town about the forty foot wooden diving tower that once pierced the skyline of the beach. And we heard stories that the bottom had never been found.

And now, to make things even more exciting, a real live Indian warrior had his own story to tell us about the pond.

"Okay, I'll ask them tonight. Maybe we can come here tomorrow," I said. I wanted to hear the story right then.

Nepon walked me to my bike and trotted alongside me as I pedaled out of Joseph's road. He stopped where dirt met pavement and said goodbye to me, in a way. He raised his paw. Let me tell you that again. He raised his paw to me, as in a goodbye wave, a salute to our newfound friendship.

My heart flew with the speed of no brakes all the way down Forest Hill. I stood on my pedals, letting the late afternoon fall air fill my lungs, releasing my soaring spirit into the crisp air and yelling from my soul for the world to hear, "I met Joseph Nipnet and his spirit friend, Nepon. I was not eaten. The Viking is a coward, a chicken heart. He is too afraid to collect money from Chief Nipnet. I am braver than the Viking."

Chapter 5

I am going to venture that the man who sat on the ground in his tipi meditating on life and its meaning, accepting the kinship of all creatures, and acknowledging unity with the universe of things was infusing into his being the true essence of civilization.

Luther Standing Bear
Oglala Sioux Chief

As expected, the gang wasn't thrilled about the idea of meeting Joseph Nipnet and hearing the story of Carbuncle Pond. No matter what I said.

"He wants to eat all of us. Not just your skinny bones," Jimmy joked.

"Shut up or I'll pound you." I had learned tough talk from listening to the Viking try to interact with normal people in a civilized, working-class American society. Besides, I was the biggest kid in our little gang anyway.

"Yeah, it's a trap," Jimmy's little brother Alex echoed.

Andy didn't say anything; he never said much. He just always had this silly, passive smile on his face, like he was at peace with the world—a healthier philosophy than most others. Scott was off in his own little world, oblivious to the topic of discussion. And he would follow along no matter where we went. My parents said he was slow – a 'retard' they called him, back when that term was considered an acceptable description of people with developmental disabilities, but his own parents called him far worse things.

"Trust me. It's okay. He isn't going to eat us," I tried to reassure them, but to no avail. So I accepted the fact that I was going alone. I wasn't going to drag Scott along, just the two of us. Besides, since I had to deliver the paper that morning, I could just stay at Joseph's after I finished the route, hear the story and then head home.

I was right. I felt safe. Joseph Nipnet was not going to eat a kid. He knew what everyone said about him anyway. Why would he tell me he

knew the stories about him if they were true?
Right?

I journeyed on with the plan alone.

"They won't come." I stood in front of Joseph's door with Nepon by my side. He had met me at the end of the dirt road, like he already knew I was coming. I had finished the route in record time, pedaling as fast as my skinny legs could carry me, so as to provide me with more time with Joseph and the story.

Joseph smiled and patted my shoulder with his massive hand. "That's okay. I will tell just you the story then."

We sat at the fire pit. Even though it was daylight and the cooler air of autumn hadn't arrived yet, Joseph lit a fire that he had already prepared. Nepon sat next to me and laid his head on my lap so I could rub his soft downy fur. I watched the fire roar to life as Joseph Nipnet started his story.

"Michael, have you ever heard of the Nipnets?" Joseph asked.

"No, well, just your last name," I answered.

"But you have heard of the Nipmucs?"

"Yes, they were the Indians that lived around here." At the time, I didn't know that the word 'Indian' could be a derogatory term for the Native Americans. Joseph just accepted it and never mentioned anything about my use of the word.

"That is right. They were a large nation that lived all over central Massachusetts many years ago and they named the large lake in the next town over."

"I can say it—Lake Chaubunagungamaug," I piped up.

"Yes, that is the shortened, white man version. The real name is Lake Chargoggagoggmanchauggagoggchaubunagunga maugg. Do you know what it means?" he asked.

"Yes, it means, 'you fish on your side, I'll fish on my side, and no one fishes in the middle.'" Every elementary school kid from town knew that.

Joseph laughed. "Well, again, that is the white man's version. Its direct translation to your language is, 'the pleasant waters of the boundary fishing place.'"

"What does that mean?" I jumped in.

"Patience, young Michael. I will explain. The Nipnets were a smaller clan of the larger

Nipmuc nation. Nipnet means 'small pond people.'"

"So, you are a Nipnet?" I asked.

Duh.

He laughed his time-worn laugh. "Yes. And we lived right here on the land of this town and around Carbuncle Pond."

Indians living right here and at the pond we swim in across Main Street from our neighborhood.

The thought fascinated me.

Joseph knew he had captured my complete attention, so he didn't look at me. Instead his eyes became fixated on the campfire. The orange flicker of the flames reflected back at the world. His mind's eye took him traveling to another time. He was there now. He was one of them, remembering his own past. He spoke into the fire.

"Before the white man came, we lived in peace and prosperity in the Nipmuc nation. We traded with the Wampanoag, the Narragansett and the Pequot. We fished the many ponds and lakes. We grew our three staples of life - corn, squash and beans—in the warmer seasons. We sent game hunting parties out into the woods for deer and turkey in the winter. Our doctors, called shamans, treated people's ailments with what Mother Earth provided, the barks, roots and berries that cured swelling, fatigue, fever, and pain. Our numbers grew. We flourished. Our people were very strong. Our people's history was just as long as any other peoples of the earth. We survived for thousands of years with our way of life.

"We respected each other and did not encroach on the other tribes' hunting lands and fishing waters. That is what 'boundary fishing place' means. An individual person did not own a piece of land, as a white man does. Instead, the land was for the whole community of a clan, or village or tribe to use. We did not take from the resources of other tribes, and they did not take from ours. We had plenty provided for us right where we lived. We did not have to raid each other and steal. We knew we had to live together with all of the other wildlife and only use just what we needed to prevail and stay strong. The important point is that we knew to give nature time to replenish her stock, so we could sustain our healthy life for generations to come.

"When we met to trade or share information, we chose a neutral meeting ground between our farming, hunting and fishing grounds. The elder of a tribe was called the sachem, like what you might call a chief. Everyone in the tribe went to the sachem for guidance, advice and blessings. The sachem did not collect all the wealth and keep it from the people, like the kings of Europe. Instead, in times of trouble, he would share his personal bounty to help those who fell on hard times.

"Wampum was our monetary system. Wampum is colorful shells and beads strung together like a necklace. We lived in houses of oval-shaped mounds called wigwams. Each of us had our role in the tribe; we shared the everyday duties so that everyone could thrive and grow."

I was enthralled, spellbound. I listened to Joseph tell the story. His massive warrior hands moved with the inflecting rhythm of his voice. I stared into the flickering dance of the mesmerizing flames. My mind's eye traveled with Joseph back in time. I could see his people moving like a television screen in the flames.

"When the white man first came, we were stronger and larger than most of them. The white man did not look as healthy as we did. They were a gaunt, ghostly white color, with dark circles under their eyes. Their teeth were rotten or missing and their gums bled. They smelled of decaying, rotten meat. They coughed, always wiping their noses. We now know that this is what happens to a human body after months of living in an old, wooden ship without the proper food - confined to a small space with bad air, and living in the same quarters as the rats and domesticated animals, infested with disease-carrying fleas."

Suddenly he stopped. He looked up from the flames and stared out across the camp into the forest, his eyes searching far off into the western sky. He turned to me. My throat tightened up; I didn't know what had happened. He had shocked me out of my own time travel trance.

Joseph squinted and in a deep, low, hoarse voice he continued. "And they carried death. Death was in them and on them. They carried it on their clothes, in their breath, and on their hands. Everything they touched was cloaked in death. The worst of all of death's angels was the red plague, the pox. Death spread like wildfire up the whole East coast of North America, starting where Columbus had landed, then heading north to New England with the trading ships and south with the arrival of the Spanish in South America. We were almost wiped out. In some places whole villages died, up to half in others. It was particularly deadly for our children. Their tiny bodies covered in red, pus-filled bumps. We did not know how to fight it. All we could do was listen to their cries for help. It would take years for our bodies to build the defenses needed to survive the attacks."

I couldn't believe what I was hearing. I looked up into his eyes but he did not make eye contact with me. He continued staring off into the western sky, as if searching for something in the past. I looked back into the fire, shaking my head in disbelief. I felt heartbroken. I had never heard anything like this before.

"Our own ignorance of the disease helped to spread it even more. Our shamans visited all the sick in their wigwams and carried it across the tribes with each visit. All the efforts of our shamans did nothing to stop the onslaught. At the time, we thought that a disease entered the body if it was not protected by the spirits, as if the soul had left the body, leaving it open to sickness. The shamans tried to allow the spirits to re-enter our bodies to help fight the sickness. But the closest belief we had to the truth was that the disease was caused by the intrusion of some evil object placed in our body by means of sorcery. Little did we know at the time that the evil intrusion was a simple, invisible, microscopic virus.

"And when your Pilgrims arrived, they found us half beaten and pox-scarred, and many of us started questioning our own spiritual beliefs."

He stopped. Looked down at me and smiled. "I think we should stop here for now. We have talked too long, and I do not want you to get in trouble. Your parents know how long the route should take, even on Saturday. I will save the Nipnets' first encounter with the white man for another Saturday."

I have to wait another whole week?

The grimace on my face displayed my disappointment to have to end the story. But I understood. I couldn't argue with his reasoning. What intrigued me though was that Joseph was being very protective of my relationship with my parents. He didn't want me to get into any trouble.

"I will tell you more next Saturday. But before I continue with the story, I have a trade to propose to you. Do you have to write a book report for school?"

"Um, well nothing has been assigned yet, but I'm sure we will have to some time."

"Good. Do you like the story so far?"

Like? Are you kidding me?

"Yes, sir, I do. A lot," I answered.

"Have you ever heard any of this before?" he asked.

"No, I've never heard anything like this. All we learned in school was about the Thanksgiving dinner with the Indians and the Pilgrims." Most of what I'd ever seen about Indians was from movies and TV shows.

"Yes, I suspected as much. Then you have much to learn. This is my trade offer. I will tell you the rest of this story. It might take several visits, but if you are patient, I will tell you all. I will tell you about the special significance Carbuncle Pond holds for our people. And, in return, I want you to write the story for your school book report, if they let you. And if you can't use the story, I still want you to write it down. And tell your friends the story. It is time our side was told to the world about early America."

Perplexed, I bent my head to the side, like a dog that hears a strange sound.

Why does he want everyone to know? What does he mean by 'it is time?' But, it's a fair trade. I need to hear the whole story, and all I have to do is write it down.

"Okay, that's a fair trade," I proclaimed.

Joseph smiled. "Wait, before we shake on this, there is more. You will need to go to the town library for part of your report. In the basement there is an older section of archived books about the early history of the Nipmucs and the first settlers of the town. You cannot check these books out, but you can sit at a table and look at them and take notes. I want you to understand what the first white man wrote from their side of the story, and I will tell you the Nipnets' side. And I want you to try to go there sometime this coming week, before we meet again."

"Okay," I said. This was becoming an adventure.

Joseph stuck out his massive hand in an offer of affirmation of our trade. The calloused, muscled paw of the warrior engulfed my miniature hand, and we sealed the deal, like the Nipnets did thousands of years ago with the other native tribes.

"You should go now. I will see you next Saturday. I will not be here on Friday, but I will leave the money for the paper in an envelope by the door."

"Okay, goodbye," I said. I gave Nepon one more rub of his silvery mane then hopped on my bike and pedaled down Joseph's road. Nepon ran alongside me then stopped when I reached Forest Hill.

I wonder where he is going? Maybe hunting with his bow and spear?

Chapter 6

The old Indian teaching was that it is wrong to tear loose from its place on earth anything that is growing there. It may be cut off, but it should not be uprooted. The trees and the grass have spirits. Whatever one of such growths may be destroyed by some good Indian, his act is done in sadness and with a prayer for forgiveness because of his necessities.

Wooden Leg
Cheyenne

That night at dinner I asked my father if he could drive me to the library. The Viking had just earned his driver's license, and in my parents attempt to win the war of raising a Viking, they would lose small battles. So, they let him get a motorcycle. But, there was no way they would ever let me ride on the back of a motorcycle driven by a Viking, and understandably so.

"Why?" my father asked.

"I have to do some research for a report for school." Now my father was big on not lying; he had pounded into my head from an early age that lying was far worse than whatever wrong you might have committed. Maybe this works when you're a kid and any offense is relatively minor. This time, I just didn't tell the whole story.

That's not really lying, right?

Besides, I knew that I would have to write a report at some point during the school year, so I was merely getting a head start on a topic, and not just any topic-a deal with a Nipnet warrior sachem topic.

"So soon in the school year?" my mother asked.

Boy is she sharp.

She always tells me that she wasn't born yesterday.

Duh. Well, yeah.

"Well, it's just like researching topics right now." Again, not untrue in the least.

"Do you have an idea of what you are going to do it on?" my father continued with the digging. My parents were the best at getting out every minute detail.

"I want to go to the old section - I think it's in the basement of the library - to look up stuff on the early history of the town."

Everyone stopped eating and looked up at me like I was from another planet and speaking in an alien tongue. They were all slightly perplexed and even the Viking had miraculously stopped shoveling food into his cavernous pie hole for a second.

"Well, that's interesting. How did you hear about the old section of the library?" my mother asked.

Wow, my parents could be relentless. I could never hide even the slightest little secret from them. Why couldn't they just be happy that I was doing school work and just say, 'yes, I will gladly take you to the library after dinner?'

I didn't feel secure or brave enough to tell them about Joseph Nipnet just yet. I knew I would have to eventually, but I just couldn't decide on the right approach. I needed to break it slowly to them, in case they had some kind of issue with it, which I was sure they would. So, I really felt I had no choice but to tell a small white lie.

"I heard about it at school," I said.

They finally accepted my story.

My father worked hard every weekday, but he never once said no to bringing me to baseball practices or playing catch with me in the backyard after climbing up and down ladders all day. He played hockey with us on the ponds on the weekends in the winter, and never once complained or said he was too tired. So driving me to the library was no big deal. Besides, I liked being with just my father. He never said much, but having him to myself was rare and special. It was quiet time amid the usual turmoil of trying to raise a Viking child to act as a normal, civilized human being. And I got to sit in the front seat of our wood-paneled station wagon. In the seat usually reserved for my mother.

When we arrived at the library, my father let me do the talking - all part of his plan to develop a responsible, self-sufficient adult out of me someday. We walked up to the front counter in the center of the library. A librarian was standing behind it watching us enter. I was about to speak when she looked up at my father and asked, "Yes, can I help you?" He tapped me on my shoulder and gave me a slight nudge forward, prompting me to speak up.

"Hi, I am looking for the oldest books you have on the history of the town and our first encounters with the Indians." I told her.

She switched her gaze from my father to me. She gave me a look that is hard to describe. A combination of confusion mixed with wonderment, like she was surprised to see a twelve-year-old kid asking about old books.

Then she smiled and said, "Yes, the oldest books we have on the history of the town are downstairs in the basement. You may take the stairs over there." She pointed to a set of stairs leading to the basement.

There was another librarian sitting at a desk in the basement room. I walked up to the desk. My father stood a bit further back this time, letting me handle the encounter on my own.

She watched me approach the desk and asked, "Yes, can I help you?"

"Yes, I am looking for the oldest books on the town and the first encounters with the Indians that lived here."

She gazed at me over her reading glasses for a long time, her glare penetrating my soul, as if trying to determine any hidden agendas. It lasted so long I started to feel uncomfortable. My father noticed her delay and wondered why she wasn't helping me so he stepped up to the desk from behind me. The librarian finally broke her trance, looked up at my father and smiled at him. Apparently my request must be sanctioned only as long as my father was with me, like I was planning to steal or destroy some ancient sacred texts that revealed all the mysteries of the world.

"Yes, I will get them," she answered. "You may have a seat at that table." Her voice had a robotic tone and beat – what zombies might sound like if they could talk perfect English. Her skeleton finger pointed to another table in the room. She opened the top center drawer of her desk and took out two pairs of white cloth gloves. She put a pair on and walked over to the table before I sat down.

She handed me the other pair, saying, "Please put these on." When she disappeared into the stacks of books, my father tapped me on the shoulder and shrugged to me, like saying, 'what was up with that?'

The room was lined with several rows of old wooden bookshelves. The light from the banks of fluorescent bulbs above projected long shadowy images of the shelves across the room.

The room smelled of old musty wood and paper - like fresh cut grass on a warm summer day with a hint of vanilla sprinkled throughout.

The zombie librarian returned with two books and laid them on the table in front of me.

"This one is the oldest written record we have of the town and the encounters of the early settlers with the local Indians. Please be very careful with this book; it was written back in the 1700s. It is mostly a collection of letters written by the clergy and leaders at the time. This other book was written much later in the early 1800s and is more a summary of the events that occurred before and during that time.

"Thank you," I said.

She walked back to her desk, sat down and started writing something.

My father whispered to me that he was going back upstairs to look at the newspaper and some magazines. When he left, the librarian's glaring hawk stare started again. I ignored it. I was now focused. This adventure was more important than some petty mistrust from a librarian.

I dove into the books, reading all I could and taking notes in the notebook I had brought with me. The oldest book was cool, made up of actual letters written by the people back then. Some of it was kind of boring stuff, but some people did record the settlers' encounters with the local Indians. They had recorded the very first meeting of the Nipmucs with a pastor and small military group led by an officer. The pastor preached to the Indians about the white man's God. How the white man's God was all-powerful and would protect the Indians too. He was a loving God, but if they did not follow his ways he could become an angry, vengeful God. The military officer talked to them about establishing trades and the peaceful use of the surrounding lands of the Nipmuc nation. Right away, I was struck by how the writers referred to the Indians as savages, heathens and poor.

I knew I couldn't read everything, so I slowly flipped through the pages, scanning each one, looking for any reference to more encounters' with the Indians. The writers of several of the letters seemed to think the most important thing was that the Indians be converted to their own religious beliefs. Their later letters discussed a dedication to enlighten the 'heathens' into the light of their God. The correspondence clearly showed how the settlers thought the best thing for the Indians was their complete conversion into the white man's faith, and the total denouncement of their old ways of living and spiritual beliefs. Some of the Nipmuc villages were converted into 'praying towns.' Many letter writers wrote that saving these poor, helpless creatures was the most wonderful thing to have ever happened.

Several letters discussed the transfer of the land in our town to a party of French Huguenots, who were escaping religious persecution in France. Those were followed by more correspondence detailing the settlement of the town and the division of personal property to each member of their group. There were also maps of the town and papers that documented the construction of certain buildings, including a church, a meeting house, and two forts for protection from the Indians.

I then turned to the newer book, which detailed fights between the native tribes of the area and the white man, as well as an attempt by King Philip — Metacomet, son of the sachem of the Wampanoag Confederacy — to unite all of the Algonquian tribes in order to fight the white man and push them back to the sea. This was known as King Philip's War. There was so much information about all the different battles, including the leaders from each side and the number of people killed.

I was so engrossed in the readings that I lost track of time. Out of the blue I heard, "The library will be closing in ten minutes." I jumped at the sound of the librarian's voice. She was standing right next to my table. I hadn't even seen her get up from her desk.

"The library is closing," she stated again in her military style, monotone voice.

I wanted to continue reading, particularly about King Philip's War. I simply responded with a polite, "Yes, ma'am. Thank you."

"Please just leave the books and the gloves on the table," she told me.

Upstairs I found my father patiently reading a magazine. On the ride home he was quiet, as usual. He asked if I had found what I was looking for and seemed content with my affirmation. I wanted to tell him about Joseph Nipnet and the story he was telling me, and the pact we made, which was the real reason I went to the library. I was excited and really wanted to share my adventure with him.

Maybe he would understand if I told him now with just the two of us here.

But, by the time we returned home, it was too late. I had chickened out.

CHAPTER 7

We had no churches, no religious organizations, no Sabbath day, no holidays, and yet we worshipped. Sometimes the whole tribe would assemble and sing and pray; sometimes a smaller number, perhaps two or three. The songs had few words, but were not formal. The singer would occasionally put in such words as he wished instead of the usual tone sound. Sometimes we prayed in silence; sometimes each prayed aloud; sometimes an aged person prayed for all of us. At other times one would rise and speak to us of our duties to each other.

Geronimo (1829-1909)
Chiricahua Apache Chief

I didn't see Joseph that whole week. I wanted to tell him what I had found. On Friday there was his payment envelope by the door. It hadn't been there the day before, so I knew he had returned from his trip - at least long enough to leave the money for me. I wondered if he was close, or even if he was watching me. Although I felt safe, that thought did give me a strange chill down my spine.

The next morning I saw Nepon waiting at the end of Joseph's road, as though he knew when I was coming. I jumped off my bike and he leaped up into my arms, placing his massive paws on my shoulder. His weight was more than I could carry, so I bent down, resting my knees on the ground. Nepon started licking my face in salutation as though he had found a long lost friend.

"Nepon, I missed you." I chuckled. Wrapping my arms around his silvery mane and hugging him. When we arrived at the camp, Joseph was sitting at a roaring fire.

They both had been waiting for me.

"I went to the library," I told him as I sat down at the fire.

"Yes." He nodded, not a 'yes,' as in 'oh, that's good,' but 'yes' as in he already knew.

I think he could tell I was excited, anxious to tell him what I had found and let me go first.

"So, what did you find at the library?"

I spilled my guts, rambling on a mile a minute, slurring and spraying the words at the fire in front of us. I told him about the strange-smelling basement room, the stack of old books, the creepy librarian and wearing the white gloves to touch the books.

Joseph laughed, which caused me to stop the rambling regurgitations. "That is all very interesting, but what did they write about in the books you saw?"

"Oh, yeah, right." I laughed back. After having only read the information once and with my very limited vocabulary, I attempted to spill out the information I had discovered. I told him about the first meeting of the Nipmucs with a pastor and a military officer. I related how the clergy felt it was a big deal to convert 'the heathens,' and the military felt it was equally important to make a peace deal to gain the use of the Indians' lands.

I continued on about the Huguenots settling our town. I told Joseph how the letters I saw described the transfer of the lands around our town from a trade with the Nipmucs and some Englishmen for some silver coins and a shiny black jacket, and how the land was then sold to the Huguenots. They detailed each family and the important buildings erected. Then I recounted the small bit I'd read about King Philip's War before I had to leave the library.

Finally, when I couldn't talk any more from lack of breath, Joseph said, "You did well. You have found much information about the first white man settlers in town, but more importantly you found out about their way of life. Did you see any specific mention of the Nipnet tribe?"

"Well, I did, but it was spelled in different ways, and they seemed to mix it together at times with the names of the Nipmuc tribes," I answered.

"Yes, just as I expected," he said. "We did not understand all of the new rules and customs of this new type of people who had invaded our lands. We knew they were here, and we knew more were coming every day. We had discussed such things with the coastal eastern tribes but had not met one of them in person yet. The Nipnets were a very small part of the greater Nipmuc nation. We kept to ourselves and only traveled beyond our land during the winter to hunt. We were not a part of the decision to trade some of the tribe's lands to the Englishmen and I know we would not have agreed to it. We did not like what we heard about the white man's ways. And we especially did not like what our chief saw in their rules, customs and different beliefs."

He said 'what the chief saw,' but didn't Joseph also say that they hadn't met the white man yet? So how did the chief see them and how they lived?

I wanted to ask, but didn't want to interrupt.

"The white man had a very different thinking about their relationship with Mother Nature. They believed they were superior to everything else that shared the earth with them. They acted as if they could do anything they wanted and take whatever they saw, or needed, or even lusted for. They did not respect the land, and they did not respect us, and to this day they certainly do not respect each of their own type. We believe that all living things are equal under the Great Father, that all living things possess a soul, and that we are all put here for a purpose and, therefore, have a right to be here. We need to sustain a balanced world, without taking all that Mother Earth has provided, all at once, until there is none left, and she is incapable of replenishing her resources.

The white man lived so differently. They put up fences, brought their own domesticated animals, and killed everything that moved in the woods. They cut down all the trees. They did not give time for the wildlife to renew itself each year, so there would always be plenty for all. They disrupted the balances of give and take, which we understood were necessary in order to survive as one earth, as one nature. They did not want to reason with us, to see our ways, to learn our ways. They expected us to change our way of life, a way of life that had flourished for thousands of years. They felt that our way of living was wrong.

"The first treaties made with the Plymouth settlers and Massasoit, the sachem of the

Wampanoags, ended with very different understandings about what was established between the two parties. There was a serious language barrier, and the full meaning of what the white men were making the Wampanoags agree to was not understood until years later, when it was too late for the tribes to change anything. Massasoit thought he was making an alliance of trade and to aid one another against the other powerful tribes in the area. But the English thought that the "savages" had agreed to accept the white man's God, total sovereign rule under King James back in England and all the rules that applied to that control—an agreement extended to all of our descendants forever."

Joseph paused a second to catch his breath. He looked deep into the fire and shook his head back and forth as if something he saw in the fire disturbed him.

"Most of the greater Nipmuc nation was afraid of the plague that had killed so many of their people and decimated whole villages. We started to question our spiritual beliefs and the limitations of their ability to protect our people. Our shamans and ceremonies could no longer save people when they were afflicted with the pox. They thought that the white man's God might save them from the diseases like He did the white man. One of the first white men to meet the Nipmucs was a Christian pastor. He taught us about their God.

"The Nipnets at first did not accept this new God. We wanted to preserve our way of life. We did not like what we heard or saw in the white man's behavior, so we avoided them. We could watch their movements and could move before they got too close. We knew these woods like the back of our hand and could be as quiet as a mountain lion. We sent signals to each other with our numerous bird calls. Each sound carried distinct meanings to everyone else in the tribe."

The more Joseph talked, the more his story sounded like he was there, like he had actually lived during that time and wasn't just reciting stories that had been passed down over the generations of Nipnets. I felt like I was hearing it for the first time from an eyewitness.

He continued on, "When the Huguenots arrived, the King Philip War was nearing its end, but there were still embers of bitterness smoldering and even more mistrust amongst some of the native tribes and the white man. The

Huguenots were nervous about possible hostile tribes attacking them, so they built two forts for protection."

"Yes, my school took us on a field trip to one of them."

"Yes, to teach you about the brave settlers, struggling to survive while living off the land in a hostile world amongst the terrible, savage Indians, protecting the white man's destined rights to everything they saw." Joseph said with a raw sarcasm in his throat. He stopped for a minute and just stared into the flames. I didn't want to say anything. He sounded hurt by what he was telling me. I looked down at Nepon lying by my feet. The massive wolf dog looked back up at me, as if to say, 'yes, he's hurt.'

"Soon after, most of the Nipmuc nation had become peaceful, praying Indians and accepted the white man's ways. Our children attended English schools for indoctrination to the white man's way of life - his language, his religion, his culture. But the white man still shot at any movement in the woods. Before they could even see what they were shooting at. A few of our more careless, younger tribe members had some close calls, when they accidently snapped a twig, or rustled too many leaves. The white man thought we had nothing in life, but before they came we had everything. We lived in a paradise. They stole, lied and cheated us of our nature and our way of life — a way of life that had thrived for countless generations."

He continued, "It is true that they considered us savages and heathens and even poor because we did not cut all the trees down and build wooden houses and we did not have farm animals. But, those of us who survived the plagues were still stronger than the white man. We were not heathens. We had a marriage system between a man and a woman. Women controlled the property of the family, which consisted of the home and any personal belongings. This property was passed along to new family members along the maternal line, which was a totally unacceptable way of living in the male-dominated society of the white man."

I was heartbroken. I had never heard nor read anything about the Indians' side of the story — especially not the Nipnet's version. All the history we learned in school was one-sided and glorified the white man to a higher God-given purpose-the white man's divinely rightful destiny to conquer the new world and all lands beyond.

"Did you read about the King Philip War?" he asked.

"Yes, but I couldn't finish the material. I want to go back and read more though. That was very interesting." I had read in the newer book that some Indians killed a father and his three children in our town and that there was a stone memorial of this massacre. I didn't know how to ask Joseph about this. And so I didn't mention it.

But then, as if he knew what I was thinking, he asked, "Did you read about the Johnson Massacre?"

Like he had read my mind.

"Yes, it said Indians killed and scalped a father and his three children. Is that true?" I had to ask.

"Yes, Michael, it is true."

"Most of the younger males, as well as the leader of our smaller Nipnet clan, did not want to convert. We wanted the white man gone. We knew too much about them and did not want their way of life. We were very happy with our own. So we felt we had three choices: change into them, run west or join the fight against them. Each of us chose what we thought was the best way for our own personal peace of mind.

"Michael, women and children were killed on both sides of the war. Some think the white man killed more women and children than the natives did. Besides, most tribes would take the captive women and children and raise them as their own. But, neither the Nipmucs nor our smaller Nipnet clan had anything to do with that particular incident you mentioned. We now know it was a roving war party tribe from Canada."

Then he stopped and said, "It is getting late. Maybe we should stop for the day and continue on next time."

"But, Joseph, please, just a little more," I begged. "You had mentioned something about Carbuncle Pond."

"Okay, but I need to be quick about it. I will start the story now, but we might not be able to finish it all today."

"Okay," I agreed.

"Michael, do you know what 'carbuncle' means?"

I thought for a second and answered, "No, I don't."

"Well, if you look up its definition in the dictionary, it will say a 'pustule or oozing sore.'

He laughed. "Not a particularly pleasant word. Yet Carbuncle Pond, a beautiful little pond, could not have been named after a pustule sore. That is the white man's definition. To the Nipnets a carbuncle meant a 'gem,' like a beautiful stone - a bright shining red gem."

The stone hanging around his neck was a bright shining red gem.

I looked up from the crackling fire and gave Joseph an inquisitive look. I was about to ask 'why,' when he spoke up again.

"The Nipnets revered Carbuncle Pond as a sacred, special place. It's still special today."

"It is?" I asked. I didn't think I could become any more intrigued by anything else Joseph could possibly tell me. But I was wrong.

"Have you ever heard of a meteorite?" he asked.

"Yes, we learned about them in school. They're rocks that fall to the ground from space."

"That is right. Well, hundreds of years ago, the Nipnets saw a bright light streaking across the sky. Lighting up the whole night like it was day. Then they saw a giant fireball, like your Fourth of July fireworks and heard a loud explosion. The ground shook and even the trees moved from the violent eruption. The tribe was in shock. Some were apprehensive about investigating the area where the explosion had occurred. But the sachem knew that it was important. He felt the meteorite was a message from the Father Sky God. After many miles hiking though the forest, the Nipnets found a large hole in the ground. At the bottom was a large rock, which was heavier than any other stone of the same size. They took the rock out of the hole and when they looked closer, they saw a red glow emanating from inside the stone through the surface cracks and crevices. The Nipnet party began chipping away at the rock with their stone axes. Inside they found a glowing, red stone. It glowed all on its own, like it had a fire burning inside it.

"Wow," was all I could say.

"But, this was no ordinary meteorite. This stone had some kind of special ability."

"Special ability?" I asked.

"Yes, now listen carefully. This is hard to accept. The stone gave its holder the ability to see things that were happening at other locations, sometimes at far away distances.

"Huh?" My face scrunched up, as I tried to understand what I had just heard.

"Yes, Michael. Just as I said, you are young and it might be hard to believe, but even now there are people in your government and your military who are secretly researching this ability. They call it 'remote viewing.'"

Remote viewing?

I had never heard of it. I didn't know what to say, so I said nothing.

"This is how we discovered the 'Great Migration' of the English and other European peoples to Massachusetts. In only a few decades, the immigrant population in and around Boston grew from the tens of thousands to hundreds of thousands. The stone showed us the vast numbers of people who were coming to settle here. It also showed us how the white man treated both our fellow brethren — the other tribes in the area — and each other.

The new influx of people from England brought with them a charter from King James which they felt gave sovereign territorial rights to whoever claimed the land first, regardless of any natives living there at the time. They treated us as less than human. They thought we were only hunters and not farmers, and would therefore not need space to grow our crops and allow our numbers to flourish. They did not understand that we knew how to sustain our way of life. We had been doing this for thousands of years before they came. We used slash and burn agricultural techniques to replenish the soil and create forest edges to sustain a healthy environment for the deer and other woodland animals. We also built fish traps in the streams and rivers.

"I will tell you this before you go. We knew there was nothing we could do to stop the rising tide of invasion and the threat to our way of life. Some of us converted; some went to war with King Philip, some traveled further west to escape the flow of the white man's wrongful destiny. We knew we could not let the stone be obtained by anyone else. Others would use it for evil purposes. So we hid it in the best spot we knew."

He stopped and looked at me. I looked back at his ancient wisdom-etched face.

"So we dropped it into Carbuncle Pond. Out in the middle where we knew it was the deepest point. You see, the pond's bottom has never been found. It has an underground spring that supplies fresh water and replenishes the life in and around it."

I was awestruck. "Is it still there?" I had to ask.

Joseph laughed and said, "Yes, it is. It is safe from the hands of the wrong people."

I didn't know what to say. The special stone of the Nipnets was buried in Carbuncle Pond, a stone that gave someone the ability to see things far away.

He called it remote viewing.

"Well, I do believe you are late, and it is my fault. You must be going home now. Your parents will be wondering where you have been all day. I am sure you have many questions, and I will tell you more next Saturday."

And then, before he finished, he added, "Michael, remember this: history is written by the victors. Whether it is the real truth does not matter. Most of America's history was written by the white man. They were the victors. They pushed us away, and made us change the personal connection each of us had with nature—a connection that had sustained us for thousands of years."

I was learning about a whole other side of the story of our country. I hated to leave. I had so many other questions about the stone and its ability, and the stone hanging around Joseph's neck.

CHAPTER 8

The outline of the stone is round, having no end
and no beginning; like the power of the stone, it
is endless. The stone is perfect of its kind and is
the work of nature, no artificial means being used
in shaping it. Outwardly, it is not beautiful, but
its structure is solid.

Chased-by-Bears
(1843-1915)
Santee-Yanktonai Sioux

I couldn't hold back my excitement over the knowledge that the Nipnets had hidden a sacred stone at the bottom of Carbuncle Pond, a stone with special powers, in the same pond we swam and fished in.

Remote viewing? You can see what is happening far away?

Instead of taking a right on Main Street to head home for dinner, I crossed the road and rode down the embankment to the pond's shore. Something inside was drawing me to the pond, like a tractor beam locked on a spaceship.

Carbuncle was just a small pond, like any of the other many small ponds in the area. But now it meant something much more to me. I just sat there and stared out over the water, wondering if the stone was really still there.

Joseph had said it was.

If it still had the powers that Joseph had told me about, and most importantly if it would ever be found. I remembered seeing scuba divers searching the pond at different times.

Were they looking for the stone?

I stayed at the pond too long. I was late for dinner. I knew I would be in trouble no matter what I said or did. Not only that, but I was late on a Saturday, even after having started the route earlier that morning. I had been gone all day, without my parents knowing where I was.

They had actually started calling neighbors looking for me, and even calling the parents of the gang. The only news they could gather was that the paper had been delivered and no one had seen me return from the route. Maybe the Viking wondered if I had indeed been captured and devoured by 'Injun Joe.'

The side door of our house entered into the kitchen. Everyone was already sitting down and starting to eat. My father didn't wait for anyone. At five o'clock, my mother had his meal on the table, and he started eating. As soon as I entered the house, both my mother and father in perfect synchronization yelled, "Where have you been? We have been looking all over for you."

Busted.

They were very upset. I knew I had to tell them everything, but I wanted to carefully, gently break all the news to them.

"I was at Carbuncle Pond," I said. This was not a lie.

"What do you mean? Did you finish the route?" my mother chimed in.

"Yes, I did the route. Then I went to Carbuncle after."

"All day? You started the route early this morning," my father stated.

I was now faced with a real dilemma. I knew I could not fib my way out of this. The circumstances were just too strange. They would never believe anything else I could think up, and I didn't have enough time to create a story, anyway. The truth was I had spent most of the time at Joseph's camp hearing the story. Even Joseph, with all his attempts to protect me from the wrath of my parents, had lost track of the time and continued on about the Nipnets' sacred stone hidden at the bottom of Carbuncle Pond. My parents would never believe that one for sure.

"Why did you go to Carbuncle Pond? Didn't you know what time it was?" my father continued.

"Um, I guess I lost track of the time. I'm sorry."

"What were you doing there?"

"Just sitting, looking at the water."

The Viking laughed, spitting a mouthful of food back onto his plate. My parents looked at one another, as if to ask if they had each heard the same thing and then they both crunched their foreheads and shook their heads, telepathically telling each other that their son had lost his mind.

"For how long?" my father asked.

"I don't know......a while."

"I went there to look for you an hour ago and you were not there."

Busted again.

I was really in trouble now.

So I did it. I said it. I told them. "I met Joseph Nipnet on my route. I was talking to him."

"What? Who is Joseph Nipnet?" my mother asked.

"He's the old Indian who lives at the top of Forest Hill," I boldly announced. The Viking actually dropped his fork into his plate of food.

"What do you mean, you 'met' him?" my father asked.

"Well, I met him when I collected on my first Friday and he has been telling me pieces of a story on Saturdays after I deliver the paper."

"Saturdays?" My mother's inflection was rising to a new world record height. "How many Saturdays?"

"I don't know. Since I started the route."

I looked over at the Viking, his cavernous mouth wide open, eyes bulging out of his head in disbelief. He was staring back at me like I was speaking in a different tongue.

"What story?" Now it was my father's turn with the interrogation.

"A story about the Nipnet Indians and Carbuncle Pond." I tried to say it with a slight edge of proudness, like I had learned something, something awesome, that they didn't know about.

"What Nipnet Indians?" My mother's pitch was rising even more, and I knew from experience that the change in her pitch triggered a switch in my father's brain. He did not like the sound of my mother's high pitch and would do anything in the world to make it stop.

I wanted to tell them about the Nipnets and how they lived right here in our town, right at Carbuncle Pond, and about the sacred stone, with the special ability of remote viewing, buried at the pond's endless bottom. I was excited to share the story with them. However, I sensed this was not going well for me. I never got a chance to say another word before my father spoke again.

"How long where you with him?" my father asked.

"I don't know." Twelve-year-olds don't have a good sense of time.

"What do you mean, you don't know?" my mother now yelled within the small space of our kitchen.

"Is that why you were late for supper?" my father asked.

"Yes."

Then my mother yelled at my father. "I don't like this, Tom. I never liked the idea of him going up there in the first place. He's too young to be going up there all alone."

"Stephen started at the same age, and he did fine," my father tried to assure her.

"That's different; he's a lot bigger. And he never stayed and talked to that old Indian for who knows how long. We don't know this man. I don't like it at all."

I looked over at the Viking. His mouth was still wide open, his eyes still bulging out of his head. He couldn't believe what he was hearing. The chicken heart who left the papers and ran, who took money out of his own profits so he wouldn't have to collect, was spellbound by the thought of his younger brother going down

Joseph's road, actually meeting him and staying and talking to him.

I held my glance at the Viking for a second longer, and managed to sneak a quick smirk from the side of my mouth toward him, sending the message, 'Yeah, I'm braver than you. I know your secret.'

Then my father did what he usually did when my mother's voice changed. The edict was declared.

"You are to just collect on Fridays and that's it, do you understand? Do not stay any longer and do not talk with him."

"But, Dad, he's okay. He won't hurt me."

"I don't want to hear another thing about it. Just deliver the paper and collect your money. Do you understand?"

"Yes." It was futile to ever try to argue with my father. So it is said, so it is written, so it shall be. My whole spirit dropped in devastation. I wouldn't directly disobey my father, but I wanted to talk to Joseph. I needed to hear more about the stone, its unique ability. I had to ask him what the Nipnets, if any others are still here. About the Huguenots, and why they had left town, all of it. There were so many unanswered questions. But, most importantly, I wanted to ask him about the stone that hung around his neck. He had tucked it away when he noticed that I had seen it.

Was this the same stone as in the story? It had the same color. Was it this stone that seemed to give Joseph the ability to know everything going on around him without ever leaving the woods?   To see everything that was happening while he sat at his camp?

Chapter 9

Do you know or can you believe that sometimes the idea obtrudes me, whether it has been well that I have sought civilization with its bothersome concomitants and whether it would not be better even now, to return to the darkness and most sacred wilds, if any such can be found in our country, and there to vegetate and expire silently, happily and forgotten as do the birds of the air and beasts of the field. The thought is a happy one but perhaps impracticable.

Ely S. Parker
1828-1895
Seneca Iroquois Sachem
Brigadier General, U.S. Army

That night I had a dream, an intense dream, as vivid as real life. In the dream I saw an old Indian chief sitting on a small hill overlooking the banks of a small pond. In his hand was a deerskin pouch that he carefully unwrapped, revealing a stone. The stone was very bright and shone with a remarkable red intensity. He held the stone in his hands and looked out over the pond. I saw his face. Deep lines of wisdom were etched around his eyes and forehead. He looked exactly like Joseph Nipnet. In the dream, I knew it was him. Sharp, crystal-red eyes sparkled from the bright reflection of the stone.

The surface of the pond lit up like a television screen. The clear, smooth water layer displayed an image, a moving image. The pond's surface became a movie. The movie showed large ships coming into a harbor of a large city filled with people, thousands of people. And more people were moving out of the city in wagons. The image on the pond showed a flood of people – white people – coming into this new land, building towns and spreading out into the wilderness around the city, cutting trees, putting up fences, toiling the soil, shooting all the wildlife. Moving out further and further, getting closer and closer to the chief's land. Then the image was gone. He stood and walked down to a canoe beached at the pond's edge. He got in and paddled out to the middle of the pond. In the middle of the pond he let the stone drop over the side of the canoe and watched as it sunk to the bottom, its bright reflection slowly fading out of sight forever.

Then I saw the native males painting their skin with the colors of the earth - the reds and browns and yellows. The Indians took their tomahawks and headed off into the woods. They arrived at a small, stockade-fenced village. It was dark; night had taken over the scene. The village had a large, open fire burning in the middle, the light from the flames trying to fight back the encroaching darkness. The chief and his warriors quietly laid homemade ladders against the outside of the fence and were over it before the people inside knew what hit them.

They caught everyone by surprise. The soldiers in the fort got off some lucky shots but were quickly cut down by the efficient killing weapons of the warriors. One shot was too lucky; it hit the chief of the Nipnets in the chest. He died from the single gunshot wound, his life-blood spilling over the ground, the home of the Nipnets. The natives rounded up everyone in the fort and told the settlers to leave this land when the sun rose on the next day and to never return. The warriors carried their chief back and burned his body on the shore of a small pond. I recognized it as Carbuncle. The smoke of the fire released his spirit into the night sky. In the morning, they gathered the ashes and paddled out to the middle of the pond. They scattered the last remains of their all-seeing chief across its movie screen surface – their leader, buried forever at the bottom of the Carbuncle Pond with the mystical stone.

CHAPTER 10

There is no death.
Only a change of worlds.

Seatkke
(Seatlh, 1786-1866)

Weeks went by without a sign of Joseph. Even Nepon was nowhere to be seen.

Maybe he went on a hunting trip.

On Fridays, I knocked on his door, but there was no answer. The money was left in an envelope by the front door. But, I wanted to talk with him just for a little while. I needed answers to my questions. I wanted to know about the powers of the stone. I felt as if he knew what had happened with my parents, like he had heard the conversation at the supper table himself. He didn't want me to get in any more trouble, so he was avoiding me.

Then I received a call from the newspaper office telling me that Joseph Nipnet had cancelled his subscription. I didn't have to deliver the paper there anymore. I felt I would never see Joseph Nipnet again.

Months went by. On occasion, I would travel down Joseph's road. The trailer and tarp-covered supplies were still there, but there was never any sign of someone living on the property.

Every night, I lay awake in the dark, listening to the winds carry old man winter home for another season of skating, sliding, and snowmobiling, wondering about it all. Winter was the gang's second favorite time of year. But, I could not get excited about it. There was too much on my mind and still too many unanswered questions.

I was astounded by the idea that someone could see what was happening far away just by holding a stone. The idea didn't make any logical sense, yet Joseph had even mentioned that my own government and military were researching this technique.

For what? As a way to spy on our enemies, I guess? Boy, the advantage that would give someone against an enemy.

I had to know more.

I thought about a lot of things, about the history of the Nipnets and of all Indians. How no one ever told their side of the story. How all of history throughout the world has been written by the victors, right or wrong, and is the only history future generations will learn. I had to keep going back until I found Joseph Nipnet.

The next day found me standing at Joseph's door. Nepon was nowhere to be seen. The place looked different, more disheveled and dirtier, and it smelled different—worse, a bad odor. I didn't sense the safe feeling that had always seemed to cover me like a warm blanket on a cold winter night.

I started to feel a little scared. I finally knocked on the door. A younger man opened the door. He was filthy and smelled bad. He scowled at me.

"What da ya want, kid?"

My heart started beating faster. I could hardly spit out the words. "The chief, I mean, Joseph Nipnet, is he here?"

"I'm Joseph Nipnet. What do you want?"

"No, I'm looking for the old Indian who lives here. I met him before."

"There ain't no old Indian who lives here."

"But, he was here. I was with him."

Joseph Nipnet - this Joseph Nipnet - was getting irritated fast. "Look, kid, like I said, there ain't no one else lives here, just me, and I've been here for a long time."

"But. . . but?"

"No 'buts' about it, kid. Now get off my property, or I'll call the cops and have you arrested.

EPILOGUE

History is written by the victors.
But there are two sides to every story.

Joseph Nipnet
1600-?
Nipnets Sachem

Over the years, Carbuncle Pond became an even more special place to me. I spent many nights camping on her shores with my friends. I told them all about the legend. They thought it was cool, but I never got the real sense that they believed it like I still do. I learned to play guitar there, sitting on the hill that overlooked the pond, writing songs to the girlfriends I brought there for those special moments of first love by the edge of the pond.

In later years, I brought my wife and our kids there, to teach them how to swim, to swing out over the water on a Tarzan rope, and in the winter, to skate and play hockey.

The Viking's attitude changed toward me after my incident with Joseph Nipnet. He treated me with more respect and protected me from the other lesser bullies in the town. I never mentioned to him that I had learned about his coward secret, but I felt he knew that I knew anyway.

On several occasions, I saw scuba divers searching the depths of Carbuncle, and I would pray that they would never find the special stone of the Nipnets. To date, no one has. In fact, word is, no one has yet to find the bottom of Carbuncle Pond.

To this day, if you look out over the pond on a full moon night, you will swear that you can see a faint reddish glow emanating up from deep within the bottom of the pond.

Oh, and I finally lived up to the deal I made with Chief Joseph Nipnet back in 1969. I wrote the story.

CARBUNCLE

It is a place like no other place,
and the stone was like no other stone.
The sun didn't have to shine through it.
It had a shine all of its own

The white man heard about the stone,
and they wanted it for their own.
So he knew what they had to do,
and the stone still lies there today.

They say the bottom has never been found,
but the white man still searches.
I hope they never find the stone,
so it can still shine on its own.

It is the jewel of the town,
I have found my peace of mind there.
Knowing the stone is safe from harm.

ACKNOWLEDGEMENTS

This project started back in the 1960s when I first heard a story that the local Native Americans who lived around our town's land had buried some kind of special stone at the bottom of Carbuncle Pond. Over the years many people have influenced my desire to finally put the story down on paper. First I need to thank The Viking, for being the best oldest brother a person could have. To, Lincoln and Jeanne Vannah for truly becoming one with nature and successfully living off the land as the Native American nations once did. To my good friend Luke Lorang, for his unwavering belief in remote viewing. To my son Ted, for listening to and reading countless versions of this story and taking up his own writing torch. To Sarah Racicot, for her creative and invaluable wordsmithing talents. To Cheryl Cory, for her superb editing and for introducing me to the world of self-publishing. And most importantly, to my wife, Diane, for truly believing in me, staying with me, and her undying patience with all of my crazy projects.

BIBLIOGRAPHY

1. Lake Chargoggagoggmanchauggagoggchaubuna gungamaugg (leak tʃəˈɡɒɡəɡɒɡ ˌmænˈtʃɔːɡəɡɒɡ tʃəˌbʌnəˈɡʌŋɡəmɔːɡ/). The lake's name comes from Nipmuc, an Algonquian language, and is said to mean, "Fishing Place at the Boundaries -- Neutral Meeting Grounds." This is different from the humorous translation, "You fish on your side, I fish on my side, and nobody fish in the middle," thought to have been invented by the late Laurence J. Daly, editor of *The Webster Times*. Patenaude, Ed (June 28, 2001). "Fabrication leaves us gasping - Old twist to name of lake comes to light." *Worcester Telegram & Gazette*.

2. Madell, Daniel, *King Philips War*, Baltimore, MD, John Hopkins Press, 2010, Print.

3. Donlin, Thomas, *Valley of the Nipmuc,* Webster, MA, The Times Publishing Company, 1968, Print.

4. Bonfanti, Leo, *Biographies and Legends of the New England Indians, Volume III*, Canada, Leo Bonfanti, 1981, Print.

5. Curtis, Edward, *Native American Wisdom,* Philadelphia, PA, Running Press Book Publishers, 1994, Print.

A NOTE ABOUT THE AUTHOR

Robert Racicot grew up in Oxford, MA where his childhood was full of adventures and legends from the outdoor paradise surrounding his neighborhood. The Legend of Carbuncle Pond is his first young reader's story. He lives in Massachusetts with his wife Diane and their dog Latty.